A Children's
Mountain Myth

Spirit Trails

Under the Mauka Moon

MW00814936

First Edition,first printing
2003

All rights reserved under
International and Pan-American
copyright conventions.

Copyright © 2003 Keiki Publishing
Text Copyright © Momo O Kai LLC
Illustrations © 2003 Anabel Baldwin

All rights reserved. Except for brief
passages quoted in a review, no part of
this book may be reproduced in any form
or by any means,electronic or mechani-
cal, including photocopying and record-
ing, or by any information storage and
retrieval system, without written permission
from the publisher.

Printed in
Hong Kong.

Published and distributed by
Keiki Publishing 1191 Kuhio Hwy. Suite 112
ISBN 0-9745646-0-5 Kapa'a, Hawaii., 96746

It was long ago
            and high above the South Seas
silky beach.
            In a mist shrouded land
known as Koke'e.

Late in the mountain night keiki children heard scuffling of little feet along the Berry Flat Trail.

High on the mist-covered mountain, in rickety
tin roofed cottages, whispers could be heard
under warm blankets, as little one's imagination
soared. They listened through bedroom screens
hoping to catch other sounds of the trail spirits.

Oh, if spirits in the mist trails night could
appear in the dawn of Keiki's dreams.
The little children might befriend and join
the secretive bands, slipping through the
mountain forest mists to adventures yet
unknown.
If only the Keiki's wish could come true the
mountain children and spirit bands could join
in the misty morning's realm and explore the
trails beyond the cottages.

Perhaps it was the sparkling water in the mountain brooks that drew the spirit bands up the moonlight trails. Or it could have been the sweet taste of wild berries found among the silver oak and koa tree meadows.

A shared plan came to the
Mountain Keiki children.

Picnics and offerings of mountain fruits
would be held throughout the Mountain Meadows
and Forests.
Along the brooks, a different place each day,
brightly colored Koke'e blankets would be spread,
with hopeful searches with offerings for some
sign of the spirit bands in the forest and meadows.

As summer picnics went forth a discovery gave a clue as to the identity of the spirit creatures.

One evening as a Keiki mother's warm apple pie cooled on a windowsill.

So it could be sliced for next day's search. Mother found the pie crust broken with small muzzle marks in the

sweet apple pie pieces.

Perhaps the Keiki offerings of berries and small fruits, along the crystal brooks over looked the spirit bands favorite taste delight'

Mother joyfully shared the news to further the summer surprise.

Now a new search began, after each picnic, little keiki's went off to find apple leftovers throughout the meadows. Again and again little pieces of apple were found under the old field apple trees.

A misty dawn, cleared in the morning sun, revealed little keiki's hefting picnic baskets piled high with sweet apples from the old orchards.

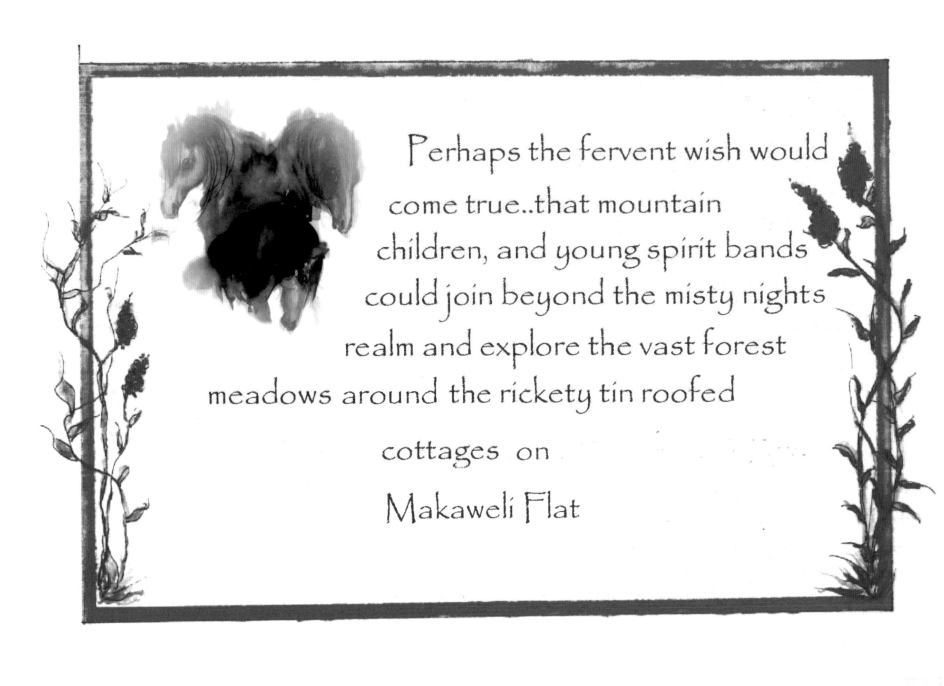

Perhaps the fervent wish would come true..that mountain children, and young spirit bands could join beyond the misty nights realm and explore the vast forest meadows around the rickety tin roofed

cottages on

Makaweli Flat

So off they hiked far
up the trail behind the
summer clearings,
to place sweet apple
offerings like those
from Mothers pie.

More excited than
ever, the keiki's
looked for barren
apple trees, placed
near the creeks by
forest people long
ago.

At last, as midsummer neared, they found apple bits under the trees, where they had placed apple offerings below barren apple tree branches.

Again and again small pieces of fruit left by small muzzles, were discovered at the picnic places that were most special.

Now, a new search began, after each picnic, little keiki's went off to find apple leftovers throughout the meadows.
Again and again, sure enough, little pieces of apple were left under the old field apple trees.

Then one day, the keiki's upon entering a meadow, heard and then saw the spirit pony band.

There in the morning
mist, stood the
spirit ponies,
with steam rising
from their backs,
as they munched
on apple delights...

Just as they appeared before the
mountain children,
they turned on scuffling
hooves, and scampered away.

Back the keiki children ran to spread the news
to all the mountain children.

No longer would they have to wonder if they
imagined sounds in the evening air. Now they
didn't need to pretend that they had ponies. At last
they knew that the deep forests of the mountains
possessed living spirit ponies.

Spirit ponies that were even
more wonderful than those
in their dreams.

Now their father's and mother's could bring forth the long held surprise that made complete the wonderful mystery.

The mystery
that held
the keiki's

spellbound

that special

summer.

One day the keiki children were led down the rugged road past the turn to their favorite stream. Then on beyond the stately eucalyptus trees they went, on the way to a high bank turn. Curiosity grew as they waited above the high bank under the forest canopy. At first there were no sounds other than the calling of songbirds and fowl,

Soon they could hear
the faint rumbling of
a motor far down the
rugged switch back
lane. Then a large
riggety truck backed
to a stop against the
bank. We watched with
wide eyes..........

As sweet muzzles rose above the trucks' box.

The little ones flared and snorted their nostrils with much clattering of hooves on the trucks hard floor.

Father stepped down from the truck with rope leads
in his hand. The spirit ponies calmed as halters
were placed on their sweet heads.

Father gave each of us a lead to hold.

Our spirit pony surprise was complete when mother and father gave us new saddles, blankets and bridles.

So summer could be filled with joyous trail rides and picnics with our spirit ponies.

Sometimes in the misty mornings
wild spirit ponies can be seen grazing
near our tin roofed cottages..and

greetings can be heard from our ponies.

To this very day, all of the children that shared this wonderous summer surprise, remember the adventures of their spirit quest, in the mountain forests high above the silky beaches of Kauai.

The quest that led to summers joy, given to them, so that their picnics and birthdays could be complete with their very own spirit pony memories in the forests and meadows in Koke'e.